I0829475

THE
SMART
ASS
BOOK OF
PUNS

YOU WANNA
PIZZA ME?!

DON'T BE
A PRICK

FULL MOON

YOU'RE BEING
IRRELEPHANT

YOU MAKE
ME FLUSH

WHATEVER TICKLES
YOUR PICKLE

YOU HAVE GOAT
TO BE KIDDING

DUCK OFF

ONE SHARKASTIC
SUN OF A BEACH

COMET ME, BRO

DON'T BE A
HIPPO-CRITE

YOU GIRAFFE
ME CRAZY

THAT FEELING WHEN
ZE-BRA IS OFF

ARE EWE SERIOUS...

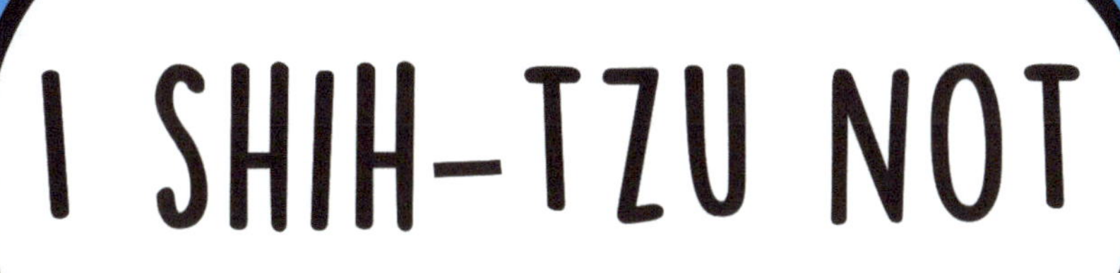

I SHIH-TZU NOT

YOU HAVE CAT TO
BE KITTEN ME
RIGHT MEOW

FOR FOX SAKE

BEARLY TOLERATING
YOUR SARCASM

YOU'RE
BOARING ME

TURDLE

DON'T BE
SO SHELLFISH

I'VE HAD ENOUGH OF YOUR CRAB

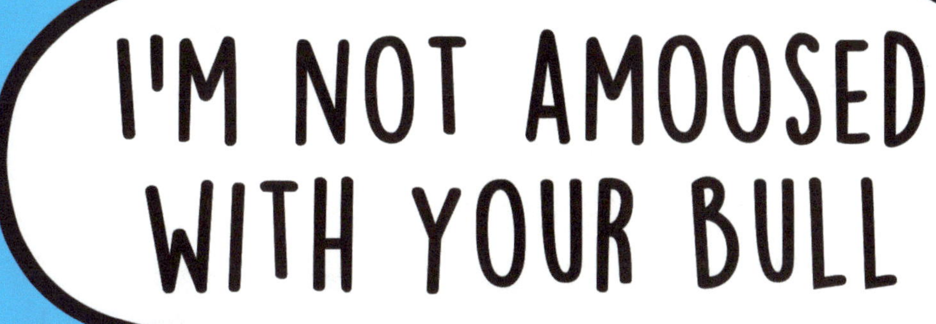
I'M NOT AMOOSED
WITH YOUR BULL

OTTER MY WAY, PUNK

TOO SOFISHTICATED
FOR YOU

DONUT EVEN...

BEACH, PLEASE

THIS IS MY
MUFFIN TOP

I'M NOT FAT, I'M JUST
A LITTLE HUSKY

BAD PUNS ARE
HOW EYE ROLL

LEFD
Designs